A Molly Book

THE HOME

By Joseph S. Bonsall

Illustrated by Erin Marie Mauterer

Ideals Children's Books • Nashville, Tennessee
an imprint of Hambleton-Hill Publishing, Inc.

To my lovely wife, Mary, who taught me all about cats and their love. To Pumpkin, Omaha, Gypsy, and wonderful Molly, for all my inspiration. To Spooker, for stopping by the Home. And to Yuri—if only we all had his spirit. Rest well in The Better Place, little gray friend.

—*J. S. B.*

For Randy
My love, my friend, my support.

—*E. M. M.*

Published by Ideals Children's Books
An imprint of Hambleton-Hill Publishing, Inc.
Nashville, Tennessee 37218

Printed and bound in Mexico

Library of Congress Cataloging-in-Publication Data
Bonsall, Joseph S.
    The Home / by Joseph S. Bonsall ; illustrated by Erin M. Mauterer.
        p.   cm. — (A Molly book)
    Summary: Molly, the youngest of four cats living at the Home, dreams of going outside and asks the older, wiser cats to tell her about the things she does not understand.
    ISBN 1-57102-123-X (hc)
    1. Cats—Juvenile fiction. [1. Cats—Fiction.] I. Mauterer, Erin, ill. II. Title. III. Series: Bonsall, Joseph S. Molly book.
PZ10.3.B6437Ho   1997
[Fic]—dc21   97-12847
                                                                CIP
                                                                 AC

The illustrations in this book were rendered in watercolor, gouache, colored pencil, and acrylic.
The text type is set in ACaslon Regular.
The display type is set in Coolsville.

First Edition

10 9 8 7 6 5 4 3 2 1

A home without a cat—and a well-fed, well-petted and properly revered cat—may be a perfect home, perhaps, but how can it prove its title?

—Mark Twain

Molly, the beautiful little calico, woke up from her afternoon nap and yawned lazily. She had been dreaming of the day when she had first come to the Home. It had been two years ago, and she had been only a tiny, weak kitten then. But Mother Mary, the wonderful humancat who lived at the Home, had taken her in. And it had been Mother Mary who had given the little kitten her name.

Molly leapt down from her bed and stretched herself out as cats do. Nap time was over, and she had to get going. As she stretched again, her eyes drifted toward the window and Outside.

"I think I'll go find Pumpkin," she meowed to herself. "I have some questions to ask him."

Then Molly hurried off to find her big, orange friend.

Molly searched all over the Home for Pumpkin. First she headed to the old couch where he usually slept. No Pumpkin there. Then she peeked behind a door at one of his favorite spots. No Pumpkin there either.

Racing down the hallway to check out the bedrooms, Molly skidded on a rug and ran *SMACK!* into Omaha.

"Watch out!" huffed Omaha. "Why are you always running? Will you grow up, pleeeeease!" he said, straightening his fur. Omaha was a handsome cat—though a little on the small side—with a charcoal and white coat. He was always mindful of his appearance.

"Cool it, Omi," Molly answered in perfect catspeak. "I'm looking for Pumpkin. I want to ask him about Outside."

"Outside!" exclaimed Omaha. "Why are you so fascinated with going Outside. I'd rather take a bath than go out there!"

"What is so terrible about Outside?" asked Molly.

"Just go talk to Pumpkin," said Omaha. "But watch out for Gypsy. Her mood is worse than ever today."

"When isn't she in a bad mood?" laughed Molly, resuming her search for Pumpkin—at top speed.

"Well, I warned you," Omi called after her as he began to wash his face, his catspeak becoming just a little harder for Molly to understand.

Catspeak, of course, is the language of cats. Cats use this unique feline language to speak to one another. It is really more like thinking than talking.

Pumpkin's catspeak was the best, although grouchy old Gypsy never had any problem expressing herself. Omaha had always had a hard time with his catspeak, but with Molly's help he was getting much better at it.

Although Molly was the youngest, she was quite good at the speak. She even understood some of the humancats' words, especially when spoken by Mother Mary.

According to old Pumpkin, indoor kitties were better at catspeak than outdoor kitties, and Pumpkin, Molly, Gypsy, and Omaha were definitely indoor kitties—though Molly dreamed of one day talking with an outdoor kitty.

Molly was still searching for Pumpkin when she heard a funny sort of rumbling coming from inside the upstairs closet. It sounded strangely like snoring mixed with . . . purring.

Aha! thought the little calico. Pumpkin is asleep in the closet.

Slowly Molly edged around the door, trying to be as quiet as possible so as not to disturb the older cat. But she almost laughed out loud when she saw that it was Gypsy, not Pumpkin, who was curled up in the corner fast asleep.

Gypsy was a huge black and white cat who, like Molly, had been rescued from Outside by Mother Mary. She was older than Molly and a little younger than Omaha. She never spoke much about her life before she came to the Home, and Molly didn't dare ask her about it. Life must have been very hard for Gypsy, and Molly thanked God for bringing her to the Home. Sometimes Gypsy was a bit grumpy, but secretly Molly adored her.

Watching the sleeping Gypsy, Molly told herself that it would not be wise to bite Gypsy's tail and run. But she just couldn't resist the temptation!

Slowly Molly crept up behind Gypsy, and . . . *Chomp!* Then Molly ran like the wind!

"Meoooooowwwww!" howled Gypsy. Poor Gypsy had been having a terrible dream, and it took her a moment to realize what had happened.

"I'll get you for that!" she yelled after Molly. Then, yawning sleepily, she added, "Just as soon as I finish my nap."

Gypsy settled back into her corner and listened to Molly giggling from somewhere down the hall. That little Molly! she thought. All that energy is going to get her into trouble someday.

Gypsy drifted back to sleep, but unfortunately the awful dream was still waiting for her.

She saw herself in a field near a river, and she was surrounded by a group of snarling cats. The leader of this pack was a huge, muscular tomcat with matted, reddish-colored fur. His broken catspeak was loud and terrifying.

"If you ever come around these parts again we'll get you good," he threatened.

"Yeah," shouted the others. "We'll make you sorry!"

Gypsy ran as fast as she could to escape the sounds of their vicious laughter. She was hungry and scared, but ready to fight for her life if she had to. She ran and ran until at last her own fright awakened her from the nightmare, and she found herself safe in the upstairs closet of the Home.

That is why I worry about Molly so much, she thought to herself. The world Outside is such a tough place for cats. Pumpkin thinks he knows all about it, but he's been at the Home since he was a little kitten, and so has Omaha. Molly may remember a little of her beginnings Outside, but she has no idea how bad it can be.

Meanwhile, Molly had run back downstairs.

"Gypsy is gonna get me back for that," she giggled. "She'll probably hide one of my favorite toys. My pink mousy, or maybe my little stuffed rainbow, or . . . " Molly was interrupted by the deep, wise voice of Old Pumpkin himself.

"Well, little one, how are you today?" he asked. "Omaha said you were looking for me."

Molly always had lots of questions for Pumpkin—he just seemed to know all the answers. Perhaps it was because he had been at the Home the longest. Whatever the reason, in Molly's eyes, he was like a big, orange king.

Molly fell into step beside the ancient one and asked, "Why can't I go Outside?"

Pumpkin stopped in his tracks. This wasn't one of the young one's silly questions that he could easily answer—like What do squirrels eat? or Why are dogs so dumb?

Gathering his thoughts, Pumpkin said slowly, "Molly, we are very lucky to be here at the Home and to have Mother Mary to take care of us. It is dangerous Outside. It's as simple as that."

Then Pumpkin walked off without another word.

Molly knew that was the end of that. But she still had a lot more questions to ask, like Why is it so dangerous? and What is it like to be an outdoor kitty?

For in the heart and soul of every cat there is a longing to run free, to play in the grass, and to hunt. Molly often watched the outdoor kitties from the window. She thought it would be such fun to join them.

Pumpkin, Omaha, and Gypsy wouldn't dare to think about going Outside. But Molly thought it was because Punky was too old, and poor Omi was sometimes afraid of his own shadow. As for Gypsy, she just seemed to hate all outdoor kitties. She growled and hissed whenever they came too close to the Home.

While Molly was still puzzling over Outside, she heard a loud voice behind her and saw a pair of hands reach down to grab her.

"Hey there you curly-tailed, little cat. I'm gonna catch you this time!"

It was Honey, the other humancat who lived at the Home. Mother Mary sometimes called him "Joe" or "Husband," but to Molly, Omaha, Gypsy, and Pumpkin, he was just "Honey." He wasn't around as much as Mother Mary, thank goodness, because he was loud and he was always picking Molly up.

Sometimes Honey could be fun, though, especially when he would play "chase." Molly loved running fast down the halls and through the rooms—Honey almost never caught her.

Molly quickly slipped out of the hands and dashed off down the hall with Honey right behind her.

The chase was on!

Omaha watched all the commotion from a comfy spot on the couch. He shuddered as Molly and Honey raced by.

Thank goodness Honey didn't want to chase me, he thought.

Suddenly there was a loud *CRASH!* from the other room, followed by a muffled, *"Oooooff!"*

Omaha glanced up from his precious nap and peeked around the corner. When he saw what had happened, Omaha laughed so hard that he nearly fell on the floor.

Honey had completely misjudged the location of the doorway and had run right smack into the wall. Now he was down on the floor with a sore head and a stubbed toe, listening to the cats meowing at him. Had Honey been able to understand their catspeak, he would have known that the meows of Omaha and Molly were really fits of uncontrollable laughter.

Molly giggled, "I guess I win this game. I think I'll celebrate with a nap!"

She was headed for her favorite nap spot when she saw it . . . an open door.

Mother Mary never left a door or window open—yet there it was. The door was open just a bit, and as Molly slowly crept toward it she could smell the Outside. She eased her head through the opening and took a deep breath, smelling a world of scents that she never knew existed.

Molly opened her mouth just a little, as cats do, in order to get the full effect of all that she was smelling. Her mind filled with thoughts of birds and trees and even—*dogs*!

Molly's heart was pounding and all of her questions about Outside came rushing back. She wondered what harm there could be in just a few minutes of exploring.

Some time later, after Omaha was able to stop laughing, he decided to find Molly and congratulate her. But when he saw the open door, his heart filled with fear.

Did Molly go Outside? he panicked.

Omaha yowled in fright, and the noise brought Pumpkin and Gypsy running.

"What is it, Omi?" asked Pumpkin, trying to catch his breath.

"This had better be good," meowed Gypsy.

"I think Molly went Outside!" cried Omaha.

"I was so afraid of this," said Gypsy, sitting up tall and shaking her head. "I guess it's up to me to go and find her."

"I'll come too," said Pumpkin. "How about you, Omaha?"

Omaha was terrified of Outside, but Molly might need him, so he stammered, "Umm, yeah, I'll . . . I'll come too."

"Forget it, guys. You'll just get in my way," snapped Gypsy as she headed toward the door. "Just pray that I find that little cat before she gets into trouble!"

Just as Gypsy's tail was disappearing through the open door, the three worried cats heard a familiar voice call out:

"Hey, what's all the fuss about? I heard Omi's yowling all the way up in the attic."

It was Molly.

Omaha almost fainted with relief.

"Where have you been?" demanded Gypsy, trying not to show how happy she was to see the little calico.

"I was taking a nap," said Molly.

"We were afraid you had gone Outside," said Pumpkin.

"Well, I thought about it," admitted Molly, "but I decided I needed a nap first." *I'm also a little frightened of going Outside by myself, Molly thought, just in case Pumpkin is right about it being dangerous out there.*

"Don't ever think about going Outside again!" Pumpkin scolded. "It's just too dangerous."

"If you only knew just how dangerous," added Gypsy as she leaned up against the open door and pushed it closed.

"But it looks so pretty and smells so exciting, I think it would be fun to go exploring," insisted Molly.

Gypsy looked down at Molly and said sternly, "Now listen. There are dangers out there that you just don't understand."

"Yes," said Pumpkin, "like huge, roaring monsters called cars."

"And ugly, slobbering dogs that will chase you!" added Omaha with a shudder.

"Even other cats can be mean and terrible," concluded Gypsy sadly. "That is why you must never go Outside. Now do you understand?"

"I guess so," Molly answered slowly.

"Okay kitties, let's go night-night!" called Mother Mary.

All four indoor kitties understood these words quite well, because they meant that it was time to go to their room. And this was the very best time of the day. Mother Mary put food in their bowls, spoke softly to them, and reassured each of them that they were loved. Then she closed the door and turned off the light as each kitty settled into bed for the night. Sometimes, like tonight, the room would fill with their catspeak.

"When you fall asleep, Molly, I'm going to bite your tail," purred Gypsy matter-of-factly. "I haven't forgotten about my nap!"

"See, I warned you, Molly!" giggled Omaha.

"You'll wake up with just a stub," Gypsy meowed, trying not to laugh when she saw Molly bury herself deeper under her blanket.

"Yeah, right," said Molly. She was a *little* worried, although Gypsy had never bitten her tail before.

"Oh, go to sleep," mumbled Pumpkin drowsily.

"Did you get enough to eat, Pumpkin?" laughed Molly.

"He never gets enough to eat," added Omaha.

"Look, he's asleep already!" said Gypsy.

Soon Gypsy and Omaha drifted off to sleep as well, but Molly still had too much on her mind. She knew that the others were afraid of the Outside and its dangers, but she couldn't help wanting to explore it. She had so many questions about the world and about where she had come from.

Then, a sweetly familiar voice seemed to whisper inside Molly's head, "Don't worry, little one. Someday you will know the answers to all of your questions. Sleep now, for God is with you."

Molly smiled and purred, then she curled deeper into her bed. Soon she was dreaming and, in her dreams, she was running with the wild ones—Outside.